The
Swamp Boggles

HarperCollins Children's Books is a division of
HarperCollinsPublishers Ltd,
77-85 Fulham Palace Road, Hammersmith, London W6 8JB

Visit us on the web at
www.harpercollins.co.uk

1

SOPHIE AND THE SHADOW WOODS :
THE SWAMP BOGGLES
Text copyright © Linda Chapman and Lee Weatherly 2011
Illustrations © Katie Wood 2011

Linda Chapman and Lee Weatherly assert the moral right
to be identified as the authors of this work.

ISBN 978-0-00-741165-8

Printed and bound in England by
Clays Ltd, St Ives plc

Mixed Sources
Product group from well-managed
forests and other controlled sources
www.fsc.org Cert no. SW-COC-001806
© 1996 Forest Stewardship Council
FSC

FSC is a non-profit international organisation established to promote the
responsible management of the world's forests. Products carrying the FSC
label are independently certified to assure consumers that they come
from forests that are managed to meet the social, economic and
ecological needs of present and future generations.

Find out more about HarperCollins and the environment at
www.harpercollins.co.uk/green

Linda Chapman & Lee Weatherly

The
Swamp Boggles

Illustrated by Katie Wood

HarperCollins *Children's Books*

To Sam Duxbury, the real Sam
(although you're much better at catching!)

Contents

The Shadow Woods...

Very few people ever enter the Shadow Woods. The crooked trees press closely together, their branches reaching out like skeletons' arms. Strange whispers echo through the quiet air, and eyes seem to watch from the shadows. Anyone who does go in soon leaves, their skin prickling with fear. For these woods are like no others. Hidden deep within them is a gateway to the Shadow Realm – a dark and chaotic world where all the mischief-making creatures like goblins, boggles and trolls live.

Many hundreds of years ago, the Shadow Realm

creatures could pass freely between our world and theirs, but they caused so much trouble that it was decided the gateway between the two worlds must be shut for good. Yet no one knew how to do this, until a locksmith with magical powers made an iron key and then slotted a gem from the Shadow Realm into its handle. The secret had been found! The locksmith forced as many shadow creatures as he could back into their own world and locked the gateway firmly behind them.

From that day on, the locksmith became the Guardian of the Gateway, watching over the precious key and stopping the few shadow creatures left in this world from causing too much trouble. As he grew old he passed his powers on to

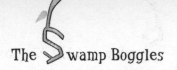

his grandson, who in turn passed the powers on to his. For hundreds of years, the Guardianship has passed down from grandparent to grandchild, and the gate has always remained safely shut.

But now for the first time, disaster looms. The shadow creatures have stolen the iron key! Luckily, there was no gem in its handle when it was taken, but there are six gems from the Shadow Realm hidden somewhere in our world. If the shadow creatures find any of them, they'll be able to slot them into the key and open the gateway, letting hordes of villainous creatures loose to cause mayhem and trouble.

Only one girl stands in their way… and her name is Sophie Smith.

1

The New Guardian

ake that, you ugly goblin!" Sophie spun round, her blonde ponytail flying, her right leg kicking upwards. She missed the target and huffed out a breath, cross with herself. Then her green eyes gleamed with determination and she ran forward again, this

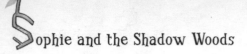

time spinning closer and lashing out faster. "Hi-ya!" she yelled.

THUNK! Her foot connected with the large white pillow that her grandfather was holding up.

"Better, but still not good enough!" he said sharply. "Do it again, child. Harder, faster!"

Sophie sighed. Since she had become the new Guardian of the Gateway three days ago on her tenth birthday, her grandpa had been insisting that she practise her fighting skills whenever she could. Sophie went to tae kwon do classes three times a week in the town hall, and loved any type of sport. In fact, she really wanted to be a stuntwoman one day, but even she was finding the practising hard going. Grandpa just never seemed pleased with anything she did.

It didn't seem quite fair. Sophie knew that if she was fighting a *real* shadow creature, the Guardian magic would make her extra strong and fast. But, without a shadow creature around, she was just her usual ten-year-old self, fighting her very fit grandfather! Sophie's grandpa wasn't like most of her friend's grandfathers. He always dressed in black, went swimming and running for miles every day and never let her win a fight if he could help it.

"Can we stop soon?" Sophie asked hopefully. She and Grandpa had been training for over an hour now, and she was getting hungry.

"Stop?" Grandpa Bob looked as if she had just asked if she could fly to the moon. "You're the Guardian, Sophie! You must train. When *I* was first chosen to be the Guardian, I trained for hours every day. You *must* prepare, or else you'll never get the key back from the Ink Cap Goblins."

Sophie shifted uncomfortably under his piercing blue gaze. She didn't need reminding of the mistake she'd made. The day before she'd become the Guardian, she'd accidentally let a goblin steal the magic key that unlocked the gateway to the Shadow Realm. Now the goblins were trying to find a shadow gem to fit into its handle, so that the key would work again. Sophie was determined that she'd find all the hidden gems before they did. She'd found one already, so at least she was off to a good start – even if her grandfather didn't seem to think so!

"And again!" Grandpa said, holding up the pillow.

Squinting her eyes, Sophie imagined that the pillow was Ug, the leader of the Ink Cap Goblins. She pictured his knobbly face, his white flaking skin, his dark scheming eyes... She ran forward, this time spinning and aiming a backwards kick.

"Take that, you stinky... *Whoa!*" She staggered

as her grandfather grabbed her foot, pulling her off balance and making her fall over.

"Ow!" She sat up indignantly. "Grandpa! What did you do that for?"

"If I could do it, so could a shadow creature." Grandpa Bob pursed his lips. "You must never show weakness or let them get the upper hand. Always expect the—"

"*Unexpected*," Sophie finished the sentence for him. He said the same thing every training session! She grinned suddenly. "Does that mean I can expect school to be cancelled for the rest of term, or Anthony to be less annoying? They'd both be cool."

Grandpa fixed her with a gimlet stare. "This is no laughing matter, Sophie." Reaching into the pocket of his waistcoat, he pulled out a black belt with a purse sewn into it. "Now, this is for you. It's to keep the gems in when you find them. I think it's too risky to leave them hidden around the house. The goblins could get in and get to them. If you keep them in this purse belt, then you'll always know they're safe."

"Unless the goblins get it off me," Sophie pointed out.

Grandpa raised his eyebrows. "But that won't happen, will it?"

"No, of course not," Sophie said, trying to sound sure.

"Wear the belt at all times," he instructed.

Sophie couldn't resist. She looked at him innocently. "Even in the bath?"

Grandpa frowned.

Sophie bit back her smile. He really didn't have a sense of humour. "Sorry, Grandpa! I promise I'll wear it whenever I can – and those goblins won't get it off me." She tightened her ponytail. "Now, where were we?"

Her grandpa held up the pillow. "Practising fighting. Attack again. Do it—"

"I know: harder, faster, stronger and without getting hurt." Sophie sighed. She squared up to him again. "Just call me Indestructo Girl!" she said wryly.

Taking a breath, she began to fight.

Deep in the Shadow Woods, Ug, the king of the Ink Cap Goblins, was sitting on a throne made out of a mouldy old tree stump, with an ivy crown perched wonkily on his large head. Black splodges covered the crumbling white skin on his squat body. Three other Ink Cap Goblins grovelled in front of him.

"Numbskulls!" Ug glared at them with his

beady black eyes. "Worm brains! The whole lot of you are a useless bunch of maggot heads! *Useless!*" Jumping up, he marched over to them. "What are you?"

"Useless, great King Ug – OW!" yelped the three goblins as he kicked each of them in the bottom.

"It's been three days since I used my great cunning and cleverness to steal the key." King Ug pulled a large iron key from his pocket and brandished it in front of the end goblin, who had a nose like a potato. "And yet I still can't open the gateway because of *this*!" He pointed to a hole in the key's handle. "Tell me what this is, Potato Nose."

"Um, it's a hole, King Ug," stammered the goblin.

"I *know* it's a hole, idiot." King Ug rolled his

eyes. "But what's so important about this hole, Potato Nose?"

Potato Nose's black eyes darted nervously. "It's… um… it's… a very *round* hole."

King Ug thwacked the goblin over the head with the key. "A *round* hole! You caterpillar-brained compost head! It's not the shape that's

important, it's what's missing from it! In this hole there should be a shadow gem. So, why haven't you found me one yet? Why? Why? WHY?"

"Um, King Ug?" The goblin next to Potato Nose, who had very big feet, stuck up his hand helpfully.

"Yes?" King Ug sighed.

"We did find one, didn't we, three days ago, but the Guardian beat you up and you let her keep it."

"*Let her keep it!*" King Ug spluttered like he was a volcano about to explode. "I did not *let her keep it*! I was forced to give it up when you three cowards deserted me! You're all useless, and so..." He narrowed his eyes cunningly. "And so, I have decided to call in reinforcements."

"Reinforcements?" echoed Potato Nose.

King Ug rubbed his hands together, making black gunge drip out on to the forest floor. "Yes! Sneaky, slimy reinforcements, who will get one of the gems for us."

"Who is it?" cried all three of the goblins.

King Ug smiled craftily. "Just you wait and see!"

2

Searching for Clues

"I don't think I'm ever going to be good enough for Grandpa," sighed Sophie to her best friend Sam later that afternoon as they sat cross-legged on the floor in her bedroom. An old leather book lay on the carpet between them. Sophie fiddled with its cover with a sigh.

"I know he wishes Anthony was the Guardian instead of me."

Anthony was Sophie's twin brother. He and Sophie didn't get on at all. Anthony hated the fact that Sophie was as good at sports as he was, and just as strong. "Anthony probably *would* be a better Guardian," added Sophie glumly.

"No way!" Sam exclaimed.

"Yes way."

Sam shook his head so hard that his red hair stood up. "Anthony would be a useless Guardian. I bet if he saw one of those Ink Cap Goblins we met the other day, he'd scream and look like this..." He pulled a bug-eyed face. "Or this!" He pulled another face, crossing his eyes and pulling his ears out. "You were really brave, Soph. You fought those goblins and beat

them. If it hadn't been for you, they'd have got away with the green gem."

Sophie felt much better. "You were braver than me," she said generously. "I had my Guardian superpowers to help me fight, but you were just you and you still fought them."

Sam shrugged. "Couldn't leave you to fight them on your own."

Sophie glowed. When she had first become the Guardian, Grandpa had told her that no one must know, but Sam had found out by accident and since then he'd been helping her. She was very glad. He was incredibly good at figuring things out, and though he might not be the best at throwing and catching things, he was the best friend in the world, and she knew that he'd never let her down.

"I think we need superhero names," Sam declared now. "Actually, you're OK. You can just be The Guardian. But I need to be called something. I'll be… I'll be…" He thought for a moment. "I know! I'll be Book Boy!"

Sophie looked at him teasingly. "Book Boy? Oh, yes, I can just see those goblins running away, yelling, 'No, no, not Book Boy! Don't let that Book Boy get me!'"

Sam grinned. "They'll tell their little baby goblins terrifying stories about me and run for their lives when they hear I'm coming! They will live in fear of The Book Boy!"

Sophie chucked a large stuffed dragon at him. "Stop messing!"

He threw it back, but she didn't even have to duck. It sailed past her shoulder and hit the bin.

Sophie giggled. "Good throw, Sam – not! Now come *on*. We have to start looking for clues that tell us where the remaining five gems are hidden." She opened the book on the floor. It was bound in brown leather with its title on the cover in faded gold letters: *The Shadow Files*. The pages were very thin, and covered with drawings and notes made by all the different Guardians of the Gateway. There was information about the different shadow creatures they'd each encountered, so that any Guardian coming after would know how best to fight them.

Sophie flicked through the yellowing pages. "Grandpa says the clues will all be in here somewhere, in case the Guardian ever needs to find the gems."

Sam frowned. "What I don't get is how come your grandpa doesn't know where the clues are. He's had the book for fifty years and seems to know it inside out, so why doesn't he know which pages the clues are on?"

"Oh, I asked him that when we finished training today," said Sophie, remembering. "I meant to tell you earlier. Every time a new Guardian takes over, the magic moves the gems, so that they're hidden in places where the new Guardian will be able to get to them.

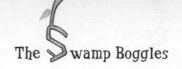

Then new clues appear magically in the book."

Sam's eyebrows shot up. "So that explains why the green gem was in Mrs Benton's cottage!"

Mrs B was the Smiths' housekeeper. She lived just down the road from Sophie, and the green gem had been hidden in her basement. They had found it on the first day Sophie had become the Guardian.

Sophie nodded. "I know, I wondered about that too. So now we just have to find the rest of the clues and track down the gems." She looked down at *The Shadow Files* and shook her head. "I just wish it wasn't such a very thick book. There are so many pages to read!"

Sam grinned and beckoned for the files. "Aha, this is where you need Book Boy. Hand it over!"

As Sophie pushed it towards him, there was

the sound of someone coming up the stairs, half singing, half chanting a rhyme:

"Boys go to Mars to get lots of cars,

Girls go to Mars to get lots of bras..."

Sophie and Sam grimaced at each other. There was no mistaking Sophie's twin, Anthony.

"Boys go to Jupiter to get a computer..." Sophie's door was flung open. Anthony stood there, smirking. *"Girls go to Jupiter to get even* STUPIDER!"

"Get out of my room!" Sophie shouted. She'd only just managed to throw her dressing gown over *The Shadow Files* before her brother saw it.

"Who's going to make me get out? Your *boyfriend*?" Anthony made a kissy-face. He looked like Sophie, with thick blonde hair and

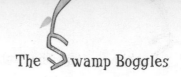

a slim, athletic build, but his eyes were different – while Sophie's were green and friendly, Anthony's were blue and smug. He put on a sing-song voice: "Sam and Sophie in the lavatory, K-I-S-S-I-N—"

"OUT!" Sophie shouted, leaping to her feet, her hands balled into fists.

Anthony jumped out of her reach. Sophie was just as strong as he was, and she practised her tae kwon do a lot more, so she usually beat him in a fight. "My pleasure. I wouldn't want to hang round with you two losers anyway!" he flung over his shoulder as he ran away.

Sophie banged the door shut behind him. Why did she have to have a twin brother like Anthony? He'd been even more annoying than usual the last few days. She knew it was because Grandpa was suddenly doing stuff with her, and Anthony was jealous. Ever since she could remember, Grandpa had spent a lot of time with Anthony. Now she knew that he'd only done so because he'd thought Anthony would be the next Guardian. But the magic hadn't chosen her twin, it had chosen her. The first girl Guardian ever.

Thinking of Grandpa's dour expression as

he'd helped her train that afternoon, Sophie straightened her shoulders. *I'm going to prove to him that I'm just as good a Guardian as Anthony would have been,* she promised herself. *Better, even!*

"Look, Soph!" Sam shoved the book across the carpet at her. It was open at a drawing of a round, squat creature with big ears that stuck out sideways, huge flat feet and enormous hands. The title was *Thunder Trolls*. But Sophie wasn't reading the title. She was looking at the four-line verse that Sam was pointing to at the bottom of the page. She read it out:

"High in an old place
The yellow gem can be found
Hidden on a dusty shelf
Strange wares all around."

"The yellow gem!" Sophie gasped, meeting her best friend's excited eyes. "Sam! You've found one of the five clues!"

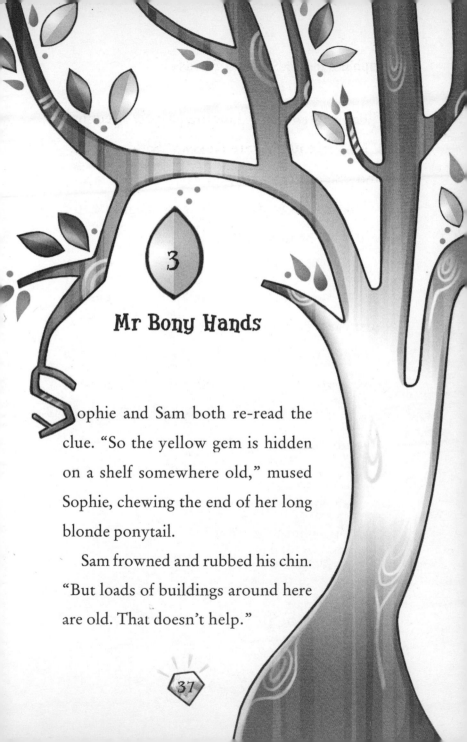

3

Mr Bony Hands

Sophie and Sam both re-read the clue. "So the yellow gem is hidden on a shelf somewhere old," mused Sophie, chewing the end of her long blonde ponytail.

Sam frowned and rubbed his chin. "But loads of buildings around here are old. That doesn't help."

He pointed to the last line. "'*Strange wares all around.*' What does *that* mean?"

Sophie made a wild guess. "Maybe wares are things you wear? So the gem might be in a wardrobe, or in a clothes shop..."

Sam shook his head. "I'm sure 'wares' doesn't mean that. I've heard the word before, I just can't remember what it means."

They looked at each other, puzzled. "I know – the dictionary!" Sophie raced for her desk, but couldn't find it anywhere. Then she remembered that she had let Mrs B have her dictionary for a jumble sale a few months ago, because she never used it. "Oh, how can we work out what it means?"

"Just keep thinking," said Sam.

Sophie thought all afternoon and all evening,

but she didn't come up with any good ideas. She couldn't even ask Grandpa about it because he was out that night and then went running in the morning. *Never mind*, she thought as she got ready to leave for school. *Sam and I can talk about it today. Maybe he's found a dictionary and has worked the clue out.*

"Have you got your school bag, Sophie?" checked Mrs Benton. She had grey hair and rosy cheeks.

"Yes, Mrs B," Sophie said, nodding at the bag on her shoulder. "It's here."

Sophie and Anthony's parents were often away from home working abroad for several months at a time because they were archaeologists. When they went away, Grandpa always moved in to look after Sophie and

Anthony and Mrs B did all the shopping, cooking and cleaning.

"Lunch?" Mrs B asked.

"Here." Sophie held up her lunch box.

"PE kit?"

Sophie nodded. "That too. I'd better go, Sam will be waiting."

"Have a lovely day," said Mrs B, kissing her.

"Thanks!" Sophie heard Anthony coming down the stairs and hastily left. She and Anthony never walked to school together if they could help it. Sophie always called for Sam, who lived on the same road, and Anthony usually cycled with his friends.

Grandpa was just coming back from his morning run in his all-black tracksuit. He jogged up to her, glancing around suspiciously. "Keep your eyes open today, Sophie," he said in a low voice. "I feel in my bones that something is going on. The woods seem quiet – too quiet. Be prepared!"

Sophie felt a nervous tingle across her scalp. "OK."

"Now, have you got the green gem with you?" he hissed.

Sophie nodded, touching the belt she was wearing under her school trousers. She could feel the green gem in there, safely hidden.

"Good. You must look after it," he warned. "And, Sophie, *don't* talk about this on your way to school with Sam if there's anyone around. Stop and think. Wait until the coast is absolutely clear."

Sophie sighed, feeling tired suddenly of the endless list of instructions. Didn't Grandpa trust her to do *anything* right? "OK. Oh, and

Grandpa…" She was just about to tell him about finding the clue for the yellow gem when an idea came into her head. What if she and Sam could find the gem on their own? It might prove to Grandpa that she was the right person to be the Guardian after all.

"Yes?" he questioned.

"Nothing," she said quickly. "I'll see you later!" She hurried away.

Sam was waiting for her outside his house, his red hair sticking up in all directions. "Hi there!" They fell into step. "Have you had any more thoughts about the clue?" he whispered.

Sophie shook her head. "I can't figure it out at all. How about you?"

"I looked up 'wares' in my dad's dictionary at home. It means things that someone sells, so maybe the gem is hidden in a shop."

Sophie frowned, wondering if that meant they had to search all the shops in town. It would take ages! She opened her mouth to say this, and then she spotted a group of year fives on the pavement ahead.

She blinked as she realised it was Tara, Ria and Daisy talking excitedly to some of the boys from their class. That was strange. Tara, Ria and Daisy were the cool girls at school, and they never talked to the boys if they could help it. But judging from the way Tara was waving her arms and talking really fast, something exciting had happened.

Sophie and Sam hurried over.

"It was totally weird!" Tara was saying. "It looked kind of like a person, a bit taller than me, but it had green skin and it was dripping goo everywhere."

One of the boys, Jamie, laughed. "Yeah, right. Oink, oink. Flap, flap. There's a pig flying by."

"I'm not lying. It was real! It was like something out of *Doctor Who*!" Tara insisted.

"I wonder if it was a TV thing – one of those pranks they play." Ria smoothed her hair

down. "There could be TV cameras watching us right now!"

"Or maybe Tara's just making it up," snorted Alfie.

"I'm not!" Tara pointed down the nearby cul-de-sac. "It was just down my road over there. Standing by the trees."

Sophie and Sam exchanged a look. As the group of year fives carried on towards school, still arguing over whether Tara had really seen something or not, the two of them slipped across the road towards the cul-de-sac.

"It has to be a shadow creature," whispered Sophie.

"I know, but it doesn't sound like an Ink Cap Goblin," Sam whispered back. "They're not green, and they don't drip goo."

Sophie peered anxiously down the cul-de-sac. "We'd better go and check it out!"

They walked down the pavement, looking around in all directions. Each bungalow was neat and tidy, bright flowers blooming in window boxes, bins neatly lined up. Everything seemed perfectly normal until Sophie spotted a large trail of slime on the pavement. She

grabbed Sam's arm. "Look!"

Sam gulped. "Either a shadow creature's been here, or there's a supersize snail in town!"

Sophie's toes began to tingle. The feeling surged up through her legs, her body, her arms and into her head. She felt a crazy urge to jump and fight as her Guardian powers kicked in. There *had* to be a shadow creature nearby for her to feel like this!

She set off at a super-fast run. The little cul-de-sac came to a dead end, bordering on to the woods. There was a footpath running alongside the trees, and a small white fluffy dog with a blue bow perched on its head and a sparkly collar was sniffing around the trail of slime. Sophie skidded to a halt beside it. The trail went straight into the trees. She picked up the pampered-looking little dog and moved it well away from the horrible slime. "I'm going in!" she called over her shoulder to Sam, who was still running down the cul-de-sac.

"Wait for me!" he called, but Sophie didn't. She raced into the trees following the trail.

Branches grabbed at her like crooked fingers, and thorny brambles caught at her ankles, but Sophie was intent on following the slime. The trees pressed close all around her, and the shadows deepened.

Suddenly she saw something just ahead of her, moving through the gloom. She caught her breath. It was a shadow creature! But it certainly wasn't an Ink Cap Goblin. It had greeny-brown skin, enormous bony hands hanging by its sides, straggly wisps of hair that looked like pondweed and slime dripping from its toes.

The Guardian powers were throbbing through her, making her feel strong and powerful. "Hey, you!" she shouted, speeding up. "Mr Bony Hands!"

The creature swung round. It was a head taller than Sophie, and wore scraps of raggedy clothes. A swampy stench like the smell of rotten eggs billowed towards her.

"You!" it said in a burbling, slimy voice. "The girl who's the new Guardian of the Gateway."

"Yep, that's me," said Sophie, stopping and folding her arms.

For a moment they both just stared at each other. Suddenly Sophie became aware of strange rustles in the trees around her, coming from the gloomy shadows. A flicker of fear rose up inside her, but she pushed it down.

"What were you doing out on the street?"

she demanded. "Someone saw you!"

"So?" The creature gave a squelchy laugh. Its teeth were very long and sharp, Sophie noticed uneasily.

She tried to sound braver than she felt. "So, stay away from the town and the people in it."

"Never! I have a job to do." The creature opened its slimy fingers. In its palm glinted the large iron key to the gateway.

Sam ran up behind Sophie, panting and out of breath. "It's got the key!" he gasped, propping his hands on his knees.

"How did you get that?" burst out Sophie. "Did you take it off the Ink Caps?"

"Take it? No, they *gave* it to me!" The creature gave a low, wet-sounding chuckle that made Sophie's skin crawl. "We've got a deal. I'm going to use it to find the gem, and then they'll open the gateway."

Sophie stared at the key. If she could just get it back, then it wouldn't matter where the gems were hidden – the shadow creatures wouldn't be able to open the gateway! She lunged forward, but her opponent was fast. It jerked the key away with a snarl as it swiped at her with long, claw-like fingers.

Sophie jumped back, surprise flashing through her. The Ink Cap Goblins had been cowardly, but this thing didn't seem scared at all! She attacked again, her right foot lashing out in a high kick aimed at its chest. *Ha!* she thought in triumph, waiting for the crunch…

SQUISH!

It was as if her foot had hit a pillow filled with water. The creature's body was so soggy that her kick didn't seem to bother it at all.

Sophie gasped in surprise as her opponent
grabbed her foot and yanked upwards, just as
Grandpa had done in the training session.
"*Oof!*" She thumped back on to the ground.

Before she could spring to her feet, it was looming over her, showing its long, spiny teeth.

"Get off her!" Sam yelled. He threw his lunch box at it. There was a splatting sound as it hit the creature and dropped to the floor.

Through the trees, Sophie heard a very faint cry. "Cutie-Pie! Cutie! Please come back!" But she didn't have time to think about it. She felt the creature's hands on her shoulders, saw its pointed teeth coming closer to her face, smelled its rotten breath. She struggled as hard as she could, but her fingers just sank into its squishy skin. Panic rushed through her. How could she fight something that she couldn't hurt or grip or kick?

"No!" she cried as the creature's teeth came closer...

4

A Lucky Escape

ophie yelled as the shadow creature reared over her. Suddenly it stopped. It pulled back sharply, looking all around it with wide eyes…

Sophie seized her chance. Rolling swiftly to her right, she leapt to her feet. As she did so, she saw the little white dog she'd noticed earlier come bounding along the path following the slime trail, the top knot and ribbon bouncing on its head. It wagged its tail when it saw her, looking like a cuddly toy come to life.

"Quick! Sam! Grab that dog!" she gasped. She had a feeling that creatures like the one in front of her would eat a ridiculously sweet, fluffy dog like that in one gulp!

Sam swooped down and scooped up the little dog as Sophie quickly got into her tae kwon do stance, readying herself for a fight. Great – now she had to protect herself, Sam *and* the dog!

The creature's eyes bulged as it stared at Sam. Suddenly it made a weird, scared, choking cry, covered its face… and then sneezed explosively.

"ATCHOO!"

Sophie quickly spun round and lashed out with her foot, trying to throw it off balance while it was distracted. But before her foot could squish into the creature, it had turned and run away down the path. It disappeared into the shadows, still sneezing uncontrollably.

"What did you do to it?" Sam exclaimed, the dog still held safely in his arms.

"I… I don't know!" Feeling equally astonished, Sophie lowered her arms. "I didn't do anything."

"So, why did it run away like that?" Sam demanded.

"I dunno." She grinned. "Maybe it was scared off by the dog."

Sam chuckled. "Yeah, right." The white pooch reached up and licked his chin with its pink tongue. "Did you scare off the horrible shadow creature, then, you big fierce dog?"

"I wonder what it was that *did* make it go," said Sophie, staring down the dark, tangled path where the thing had vanished. "And what kind of creature it was."

Sam nodded. "We'd better check *The Shadow Files* straight after school. We can ask your grandpa too. He might know."

Sophie's heart sank. What on earth would Grandpa say when he heard that she'd had a chance to get the key back and hadn't managed it? Or that the creature had nearly bitten her? She really didn't want to have that conversation at all!

Just then there was another faint cry through the trees. "Cutie-Pie! Cutie-Pie! Come back!"

Sam rolled his eyes. "*Cutie-Pie?*"

"That must be the dog's owner," said Sophie. "Come on, let's take it back." She'd be glad to get out of here, she realised, glancing around her. The woods seemed to be closing in on them somehow. It felt like dozens of eyes were watching them.

They hurried back down the path. An old lady with grey hair was standing on the edge of the wood, looking very anxious as she called into the trees. She exclaimed in delight when she saw them. "You found my Cutie-Pie!"

"Yes. He's OK," said Sam, putting the dog

down. "He just followed a scent into the trees."

Cutie-Pie bounded up to his owner and put his paws up on her legs.

"Thank you so much for bringing him back, dears," said the old lady, picking the little dog up. "I had such a fright when I realised he'd gone! You naughty little Cutie," she scolded, tapping the dog's nose. "Come on, I'll give you a nice bowl of chicken for breakfast." Looking very relieved, she carried the dog away.

Sam looked at his watch. "We should get to school."

Sophie took a breath. After all the excitement it was hard to imagine just going to school like normal, but they'd be late if they didn't hurry. "Let's just hope we don't meet any more shadow creatures on the way!" she said.

It was too risky to talk about what had happened while they were at school, but as soon as the day was over with, Sophie and Sam hurried back to her house to check out *The Shadow Files*.

Mrs B opened the door for them. "How was school?" she asked cheerfully.

"OK, thanks," said Sophie as they went inside. She swallowed, glancing around her. "Is, um… Grandpa in?'"

"No, he's at Jack Badgett's shop," said Mrs B. She shut the door behind them.

Sophie let out a relieved sigh. Jack Badgett was Grandpa's friend, and when they got talking they chatted for hours. At least that meant that she didn't have to tell him what had happened, just yet!

"Come on, let's go upstairs," she said to Sam as they started to take their shoes off.

Mrs B's blue eyes were twinkling. "First, come into the kitchen. I bought you a present today!"

"Oh." Sophie tried to look pleased. Mrs Benton was wonderful, and she often bought Sophie presents to make up for the things Grandpa had always treated Anthony to, but the trouble was she had a strange idea of what kind of things Sophie might like. When Sophie was little, Mrs B had bought her endless princess dresses, when all Sophie had wanted was to dress up like a knight or Spider-Man. Just recently, Mrs B had started buying Sophie hair and make-up sets, but although Sophie had waist-length blonde hair, she could never be bothered with trying to put bows or slides in.

Still no matter how awful Mrs B's presents were, Sophie couldn't bear to hurt her feelings, so she always had to pretend that she liked them.

"It might not be *that* bad," Sam whispered, reading her thoughts.

Anthony's voice floated out of the kitchen. "Oh, let me tell her! Let me!" he was begging Mrs B.

"Something tells me it's going to be bad," Sophie muttered, her heart sinking as she heard the delight in her brother's voice. She braced herself and went into the kitchen.

Mrs B was holding out a plain white plastic bag. "Here it is, duckie!" she beamed. "I was in Jack's shop this afternoon, and he's just got a job lot of them in. He was telling me how much his granddaughter, Daisy, loves hers. All the girls at school are playing with them, apparently! You really should have said."

Sophie felt a flicker of horror as she thought about what all the girls in her class had been playing with for the last two weeks. No, surely Mrs B couldn't have bought her a... a...

"It's a *Fluffy*!" Anthony crowed, unable to keep quiet a second longer.

Sophie opened the bag and peered inside. Big blue eyes stared back at her out of a round plastic baby face. She cautiously took the creature out of the bag. It had a tiny rosebud mouth, long eyelashes and a body shaped like a fat baby, but it was covered in fluffy pale pink fur.

"Press the button on its tummy – go on!" Mrs B urged.

Reluctantly, Sophie did.

64

"Mama!" it said in a voice like a dalek. It blinked its eyes and stared at her. "Feed me!"

"It even comes with its own bottle," cooed Mrs B. "Well, what do you think, Sophie?"

Sophie thought the Fluffy was the grossest, yuckiest thing she had ever seen in her life, but she forced herself to smile. "Thanks, Mrs B. It's... it's great."

She saw the horror and sympathy on Sam's face as she gingerly held the Fluffy at arm's length. It was still staring at her with its ridiculously big eyes. "Mama! Baby hungwy! Feed me, Mama!"

Anthony chortled. "Go on, sis! Feed it!"

Cringing inside, Sophie took the bottle out of the bag and pressed it to the Fluffy's lips. Immediately it began to make slurping, sucking noises. Then it blinked again. "Wanna cuddle! Wanna kiss-kiss. Wanna..." It seemed to pause and look at her. "WEE-WEE!"

Sophie's heart dropped like a stone as Anthony and Sam both collapsed laughing, united for once. How *could* Mrs B have given this to her? There was no way she could take it into school! She could just imagine how the boys who she played football with at break time would laugh at her too.

"Honestly, you two!" huffed Mrs B at Sam and Anthony. "Don't laugh at Sophie's lovely present."

Anthony and Sam sniggered.

Mrs B frowned. "That's enough. Now come and help me get the ironing things out. I really must get it done before teatime. Sophie and Sam, can you fetch the laundry basket, iron and starch spray from the utility room, and Anthony, can you get the ironing board out for me, please?"

Anthony sighed, but Sophie and Sam helped willingly as Mrs B fetched biscuits and drinks for them all.

"What's this spray for?" Sam asked curiously,

taking the iron and starch spray to Mrs B. "My mum and dad don't spray our clothes when they iron."

"Starch, duckie?" Mrs B said, plugging the iron in. "It takes out the creases and stiffens the clothes." She chuckled. "When I was a girl I used to use so much starch on my father's shirts they could stand up all on their own. Now, I'd better get some hangers and get started."

Looking interested, Sam started to read the back of the can.

"Weirdo alert!" Anthony muttered under his breath as Mrs B bustled out of the room to fetch the hangers. "Only *you* could be interested in some dumb ironing spray, Sam."

Sam flushed, quickly putting the spray down again.

"Shut up!" Sophie hissed.

Anthony grinned. "Why? What will you do? Hit me with your ickle-wickle Fluffy?"

Sophie saw the glee in his face. She started towards him, but he was too quick for her. Still chuckling, he grabbed a biscuit and darted out of the room.

"Never mind him," muttered Sophie to Sam. "Come on, let's go and check out *The Shadow Files.*"

Grabbing their drinks and biscuits, they went up to Sophie's room and closed the door. Pulling *The Shadow Files* out from under her bed, Sophie opened the book up and Sam quickly started leafing through.

"No, not a Marsh Goblin," he muttered. "Or a Slime Troll, or a Snail Gnome... Yes!" he exclaimed suddenly. "Look, here it is! I thought I'd seen one in here."

Sophie stared. The creature on the page Sam was holding out looked exactly like the thing they had seen that morning!

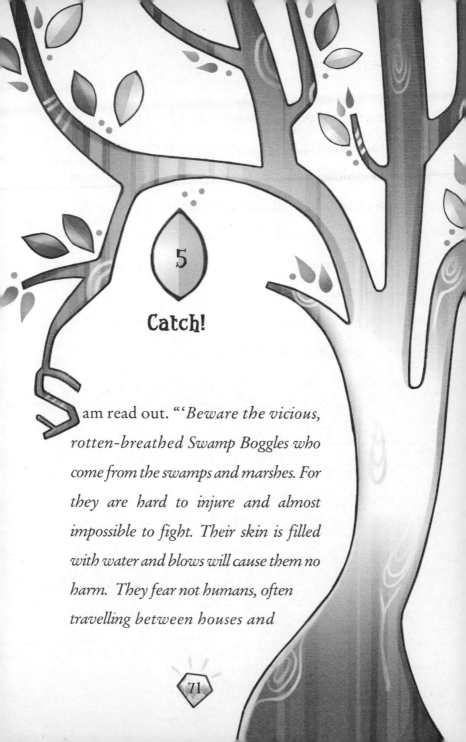

5

Catch!

am read out. "'*Beware the vicious, rotten-breathed Swamp Boggles who come from the swamps and marshes. For they are hard to injure and almost impossible to fight. Their skin is filled with water and blows will cause them no harm. They fear not humans, often travelling between houses and* buildings using drains and underground waterways.'"

Sophie listened with mounting dread. "That's really not good. If they can travel through the town, they'll be able to find the gems. Because the key glows whenever it's near one of them, remember?"

"There's another note here." Sam pointed to the bottom of the page. "It looks like your grandpa's handwriting. 'Fighting a Swamp Boggle'," he read out. "'See Fighting Slime Trolls and Marsh Goblins. Many similarities. Same things may work?'"

Sam quickly found the Slime Troll page.

"What does it say?" Sophie looked at him hopefully.

"'To fight a Slime Troll, one must first dry out their skin through use of wind or heat for then

they will become vulnerable to blows.'" Sam looked at Sophie. "We could try that on the Swamp Boggle!"

"But how?" said Sophie.

Sam scratched his head; Sophie could sense his brain whirring. "Let's see… we could rig up a massive fan. It would need to be on wheels so we could transport it, and battery powered of course, so it wouldn't need a cable, and then..."

"Whoa!" Sophie broke in. "Where are we going to get a massive fan from, let alone a battery pack to power it?" She sighed. "I wonder if the page on Marsh Goblins is any more use."

Sam flicked the pages. "Here it is! '*When a Marsh Goblin is terrified it will dissolve into a puddle of water and never recover.*'" He looked up at Sophie. "So we have to scare one to death!"

Sophie raised her eyebrows. "Let me see. Hands the size of bicycle wheels, teeth like a ninja piranha, body that can't be hurt. Oh, yeah, a Swamp Boggle is going to be so easy to terrify!" With a groan, she got up and went restlessly to the window, looking across the lawn to where the woods pressed up against the fence. The washing was fluttering on the line, but then another movement caught her attention. What was that? She peered more closely at the trees. Surely it wasn't…

But it was.

"Sam!" she hissed. "Look! By the fence!"

Sam joined her and followed her gaze. "Oh, no – it's the Swamp Boggle!" he said in dismay.

They watched as the Swamp Boggle stared over the fence towards the house.

"Sophie!" said Sam suddenly. "What if Mrs B goes into the garden to get more washing in?"

They looked at each other in horror and the next minute were both racing down the stairs.

"We're just going outside!" Sophie gabbled as she and Sam ran past Mrs B, who was still standing at the ironing board. "Stay here! Don't go out!"

"Oke-dokey. But could you bring the rest of the washing in for me, then, please, duckies?" Mrs B didn't look surprised. She was used to Sophie and Sam's games.

Only this time it wasn't a game! As Sophie got outside and saw the Swamp Boggle, she felt the familiar feeling of power surge through her. She whizzed to the bottom of the garden. "Stop right there!" she commanded as the Swamp Boggle put its hands on the fence.

The Swamp Boggle gave a burbling hiss. "You again!"

"Yes, me!" Sophie breathed slowly and deeply, like her tae kwon do teacher had taught her. It kept her calm, which she really needed right then. She had no idea how she was going to fight this thing. "This is my house. Go away!"

"No," the creature gurgled.

"Then take this, you great big slime ball!" Sophie leapt into the air and felt her feet splat against the creature's shoulders. The Swamp Boggle hissed, showing off his set of spiny, giant teeth.

"Soph, wait! I've got an idea!" Sam burst out.

Sophie didn't have time to ask what it was – the thing was lunging at her with its long bony fingers. As she dodged, she saw Sam run off. What was he doing? Suddenly she felt very alone.

The Swamp Boggle lashed out again. Sophie raced round behind it and jumped into the air, whipping her body sideways and kicking out hard. Left foot… right foot. *Splat! Splosh!*

The Swamp Boggle stumbled forward slightly, but then swung round again, unhurt.

Great – *that* had really worked. Sophie glanced about. Where was Sam?!

"We will find the hidden gems, little girl!" hissed the Swamp Boggle.

We? thought Sophie. At the same moment there was a laughing sound behind her, like swamp mud glooping. Two more Swamp Boggles emerged from the trees!

Sophie's heart flipped in her chest. There were three of them now – how was she ever going to fight them all? Straightening her shoulders, she tossed her ponytail back. Never mind how – she had to try!

She lunged forward, but the first Swamp Boggle – the chief – lifted her into the air as easily as if she was a doll. "Let go of me!" she yelled.

"With pleasure," snarled the boggle, throwing her over the fence. She crashed on to the ground, but managed to roll over, breaking her fall. The other two Swamp Boggles charged towards her with a roar. Only slightly winded, Sophie leapt to her feet. She ducked and dodged, avoiding one set of fingers, swerving from another set of teeth, seeing the first Swamp Boggle climbing back over the fence towards her too.

The Swamp Boggles made a circle round her and began to close in. She looked frantically from side to side.

"Sophie! Catch!"

Sam appeared at the fence, holding up a blue and yellow spray can. What was *that*? Sophie stared in bewilderment as he threw it towards her. It soared into the air. Using all her Guardian agility, Sophie shot upwards, just as the Swamp Boggles pounced on the space where she'd been standing a split second before. They squelched into each other, falling into a slimy heap.

Sophie landed on the grass behind them, holding the can.

"Spray them with it, Soph!" Sam called.

Sophie had no idea why she should spray them, but she trusted Sam absolutely. Pressing down the nozzle hard, she aimed the spray at the boggles. A white cloud hissed out, and Sophie smelled the familiar sweet scent of Mrs B's starch.

"Argh! Ow! Ouch! Urgh!" The Swamp

Boggles started hopping around as the mist covered them, hardening and stiffening their slimy skin.

"Yes! Try fighting them now!" shouted Sam.

Sophie leapt at the first one, kicking out with her right foot. This time as her foot made contact there was a satisfying cracking sound.

"Yargh!" the chief Swamp Boggle yelped.

Hope spiralled through Sophie, spurring her on. "Hi-YA!" she shrieked, spinning round again and attacking with kick after kick. Smack! Crash! Thump!

The Swamp Boggles had had enough. With a howl of dismay they charged back into the woods, their dry skin not leaving even a trace of their usual gooey slime trail.

Sam punched the air. "Fear the starch!" he yelled at them.

Sophie grinned at him, her green eyes sparkling. "Now, *that* was cool!" She shook her head. "Whatever made you think of using the starch spray?"

"It just came to me!" Sam exclaimed. "I was thinking we need something to make them less squishy so your kicks would hurt them, and then I remembered Mrs B saying how starch used to make her dad's shirts really stiff. I had to try it!"

Sophie leapt back over the fence and high-fived him. "Well, it was wicked! I owe you one, Book Boy."

Sam raised an eyebrow. "So you'll do me a favour in exchange?"

"Anything!" Sophie promised.

Sam glanced round to where Mrs B had just come out into the garden. "OK then... *you* can tell Mrs B that we've just used up all her starch!"

The Yellow Gem

rs B's usual cheerful smile faded slightly when she heard that Sophie and Sam had used up all her starch.

"I'm sorry. I'll buy you some more," Sophie promised.

"But what on earth were you doing with it?" Mrs B looked astonished.

Sophie could just imagine what

Mrs B would say if she told her the truth. *Having a fight with three savage Swamp Boggles who seemed to want to rip my head off.* "Just messing around," she said quickly. "I'm really sorry, Mrs B. We'll go and buy you some more right away."

Sophie grabbed her school bag from her room and put *The Shadow Files* inside it.

"If you're going out don't forget your Fluffy!" Anthony said, waving it as he came over to her.

"Wanna cuddle!" it announced.

Sophie forced a smile as Anthony pushed it into her hands. "Thanks," she said through gritted teeth.

"Lovely!" beamed Mrs B. "Thank you, Anthony. That was very thoughtful of you."

As Mrs B turned away, Sophie pulled a face

at her twin. He smirked back. Shoving the Fluffy deep into her bag, Sophie opened the door. "Come on, Sam."

"At least we know how to fight Swamp Boggles now," she said as they walked towards the shops on the High Street. "If we see them looking for gems, then we can just spray them with starch!"

Sam nodded. "The trouble is what happens when we're not around," he pointed out. "If they can travel underground like it says in *The Shadow Files*, then they'll be able to get all round town."

Sophie bit her lip. It was true. She and Sam couldn't watch them every second of the day and night. "What are we going to do?"

Sam frowned. "Plan A: we scare them so much they then dissolve into puddles of water."

"No good. They're not frightened of anything!" said Sophie.

"Plan B: we find all the gems before they do."

"Easier said than done," Sophie commented. "What's Plan C?"

Sam looked worried. "Think of another plan!"

Reaching the supermarket, they bought three cans of starch spray, using most of Sophie's pocket money. "I wonder if Grandpa will pay me back," she said glumly, gazing into her almost-empty purse.

Sam looked across the High Street. "Should we go and see him? Mrs B said he's at Mr Badgett's. We could go and tell him what's been going on."

Sophie winced. She still wasn't looking

forward to telling Grandpa that she had let the boggles get away with the key! "Maybe I'll talk to him tonight…"

But it was too late; Sam was already crossing the road.

Mr Badgett's shop – *Anything Goes* – was up a small alley, just off the High Street. It was one of the oldest buildings in the town and had a twisting, winding staircase and lots of little rooms, including a cellar and an attic. Mr Badgett sold all sorts of things, both new and old, and sometimes he paid Sam and Sophie to unpack boxes for him and tidy shelves.

The bow window at the front of the shop was packed full of things. Sophie grimaced at the sight of three brand-new Fluffies on an old pine rocking chair. "Do we really have to go in?" she said reluctantly.

Sam didn't answer; he stood staring up at the sign above the shop door as if he couldn't believe his eyes. "Look!" he pointed. "I *knew* I'd seen the word before!"

Sophie followed his gaze. "*Anything Goes, stockists of wares old and new, big and small...*" She stopped, realising. "Wares," she breathed.

Sam nodded. "And do you remember the rest of the clue?" He recited it:

"*High in an old place*
The yellow gem will be found
Hidden on a dusty shelf
Strange wares all around."

Hope leapt through Sophie. "Mr Badgett sells strange wares. Do you think, maybe... maybe the yellow gem is hidden in here?"

"Come on!" Sam pushed open the door and they ran into the shop.

Mr Badgett and Grandpa were in the front room. Mr Badgett was a tall, skinny man with long grey hair and a grey beard, and he wore a faded checked waistcoat and brown trousers.

Grandpa looked very different with his closely-cropped grey hair, tanned arms and black clothes, but the two men had always been good friends.

"Well, look who it is!" smiled Mr Badgett as Sophie and Sam came in. "My two favourite helpers. Have you come to earn some more pocket money, then?"

"No, not—" Sophie started to say, but she broke off as Sam elbowed her.

"Yes, please. Have you got any shelves that need tidying up, Mr Badgett?" He shot a glance at Sophie. "Maybe some *high* shelves."

Sophie realised what he was doing. Tidying up would be a perfect excuse to look around!

"Yes, of course. Why don't you start through there?" Mr Badgett pointed to the next-door room, which was full of household things. He fetched a couple of dusters and some polish from under the counter. "And the toy room needs a good tidy too. Those Fluffies are selling like hot cakes! You could bring a few more down from the storeroom for me."

Grandpa gave Sophie a sharp look. "Haven't you got other things you should be doing? More important things?"

She gave him a meaningful stare. "No, this is *very* important, Grandpa. I think we really should do these shelves for Mr Badgett. Please could you ring Mrs B and let her know where we are, though, so she doesn't worry?"

Grandpa frowned and then understanding seem to dawn in his eyes. He nodded quickly. "Very well, I'll ring Mrs B. You run along, Sophie."

Sophie hurried after Sam. "I'm sure he

knows something's going on. Wouldn't it be brilliant if we could find the yellow gem and show it to him on the way home?"

"It would!" Sam looked around at the cupboards and shelves piled high with crockery and glasses, the jumble of brooms and mops, bins and storage boxes. "But finding it isn't going to be easy."

Sophie followed his gaze. How could they possibly find one tiny gem amongst all these things? She took a deep breath. There was only one thing to do. "Time to get tidying!" she said.

An hour later the two rooms looked much better, but they still hadn't found the yellow gem. "Let's get those Fluffies down from the storeroom for Mr Badgett," said Sam. "And then we can start looking upstairs."

The attic storeroom was all the way up the creaking wooden staircase – a low-ceilinged room with things piled everywhere: old shop mannequins without arms, rails of clothes, shelves stacked high, a barrel brimming over with sporting equipment. And, in the corner, a massive mountain of Fluffies in their boxes, covered by an old sheet.

Sophie grabbed three Fluffies from under the sheet. "Should we take these downstairs?"

Sam didn't reply. He was staring around him. "*'High in an old place... Hidden on a dusty shelf.'* Sophie!" he said suddenly. "I bet the gem's in this room!"

Sophie's stomach flipped. Maybe he was right. "Let's ask Mr Badgett if we can tidy up here!"

They raced back downstairs. Mr Badgett was

just cashing up the till and Grandpa was standing by the front door. "Are you ready to go, you two?" he said. "Jack's shutting up now."

"Shutting up?" Sophie's heart sank.

"Yes, thank you for your help." Mr Badgett handed Sophie and Sam a two-pound coin each from the till. "You've done a wonderful job."

Sam shot Sophie a look. "Can we come back tomorrow after school and tidy the attic?" he blurted out.

"Why – of course you can," said Mr Badgett, looking surprised. "It could certainly do with a good sort-out up there."

Sophie saw Grandpa's eyes narrow thoughtfully as he gazed at them. "Tell you what, Jack," he said suddenly. "Why don't you and I go for a quick drink and leave Sophie and

Sam here to do a bit more tidying? I've got my mobile so they can ring me if they need us. We can lock the front door, but leave the back door unlocked in case they need to get out in an emergency."

"Oh, yes. Please!" Sophie begged Mr Badgett.

"Well, it does seem a shame to waste such enthusiasm!" laughed Mr Badgett. "If you think it's all right, then, Bob. Of course they can stay. We'll just be half an hour or so."

He unlocked the back door that led on to a walled courtyard. There were stone statues all round it, and a dry fountain in the middle.

"No one can get in here, the walls are too high," he explained. "And we'll make sure we lock the front door on our way out."

"Thanks, Mr Badgett!" Sophie's, eyes gleamed. "Come on, Sam! Let's go back upstairs."

They shoved the cleaning things in Sophie's backpack and pounded up the staircase. Back in the attic, they started taking things off the shelves as fast as they could. Clouds of dust flew up and soon they were both sneezing. Sam opened up the stepladder and began to check out the top shelves, handing things down to Sophie.

"Some of this stuff looks like it's been here forever. These are ancient!" He handed her down four faded boxes with hairdryers in. "And look at this! Gross!" He handed her a sickly sweet painting of a little girl with a cute kitten in her arms. "Lucky Mrs B hasn't seen this or she'd probably have bought it for your bedroom wall!"

Sophie shuddered. He was right. "Any sign of the gem?"

"Not yet." Sam gave Sophie a stack of old books. Dust flew off them, making her cough. "Are you OK?" he asked in concern as she choked and spluttered.

Sophie felt like she had just swallowed the contents of a Hoover. "I'm going to get some water!"

She went down to the toilet on the first-floor landing. Splashing some water from the sink over her face, she washed her hands and then caught some water in her palms, gulping it down and swilling the dust in her throat away.

As she dried her hands, she looked out of the window down on to the walled courtyard. She frowned. Something down there was moving. The fountain was turned off, but the drain cover on the ground underneath it was slowly lifting up!

Sophie felt her mouth drop open. As she watched, the drain cover fell with a clatter and a slimy head poked out.

"No!" she gasped.

A Swamp Boggle leapt out from the drain and stood in the courtyard. Pulling the iron key out of its clothing, it held it up towards the building. Even from high above, Sophie could see that it was glowing with a yellow light.

She remembered how the key had glowed with a green light when it had been near the green gem a few days ago. The Swamp Boggle must be using it to try to find the gem!

Two other Swamp Boggles came climbing out behind their leader. Goo dripped from them on to the courtyard. Rubbing their slimy hands, they headed towards the unlocked back door!

7

Under Attack!

ophie raced up to the attic. "Sam!"

"Sophie, look!" He had got down from the ladder and was holding something in his hand. "I've—"

Sophie interrupted him. "The Swamp Boggles are here!"

101

Sam's face paled. "Where?"

"Outside! I saw them climb out of the drain in the courtyard! They had the key, and it was glowing. They know the gem is somewhere in this shop!"

"It is." Sam opened his fingers. Sophie's eyes became the size of dinner plates as she saw the glowing yellow jewel in his hand. "I just found it, on the top shelf!" he said.

"Oh, wow!" Sophie was torn between relief and panic. "That's brilliant! Now we just have to somehow get it away from the Swamp Boggles. Maybe they haven't come in yet." She grabbed Sam and started pulling him to the staircase. "We might still be able to escape!"

But as they reached the top of the stairs, Sophie knew it was too late. Power tingled through her and she heard the Swamp Boggles below. *Squish! Squelch!* Their soggy feet moved across the carpet as they searched for the gem. "Where is it?" one of the boggles grumbled.

"It's got to be here somewhere," said another with a very hissy voice.

"And when we find it, we'll take it to Ug and open the gateway. Har... har... har..." Sophie recognised the chief boggle's laugh.

She and Sam stared at each other and then slipped away as quietly as they could. They crept back to the attic. "We're trapped!" Sam whispered.

Sophie looked around the room. "What about a window?" But there weren't any in the attic. She took a deep breath. "OK, so… we're going to have to fight them!"

Sam paced up and down. "How are we going to do this?" he muttered almost to himself. "I know! Let's hide and lie in wait. The key will lead the boggles up here. When they come in we'll attack them with the starch cans, then hopefully you can fight them off and we'll get past them and escape."

"Only one problem," Sophie pointed out. "The starch is downstairs!"

They exchanged dismayed looks.

"OK," Sam ran a hand through his hair. "Think again. What can we do?" His eyes fell on the pile of dusty hairdryers. "I know! We can use those to dry the boggles out!"

"Great idea!" Sophie gasped.

They quickly took the four hairdryers out of their faded boxes and plugged them into the wall. Then Sophie took the gem from Sam and slipped it into her purse belt along with the green one. She just hoped the boggles wouldn't realise the gems were on her!

Shoving the thought away, she picked up a hairdryer in each hand and waved them about like pistols. "Hairdryers at dawn!" she said in a small voice.

Sam only gulped in reply.

Sophie sympathised. Even with her Guardian powers surging through her, her heart was racing with fear. Then her scalp prickled as down below she heard a slow squelching noise on the stairs. The Swamp Boggles were coming!

"Come on, we've got to hide!" she said. She and Sam ducked behind one of the shelves, holding the hairdryers tightly. After a few moments, Sophie heard the Swamp Boggles's voices on the other side of the door.

"Look at the way the key's glowing!" chortled the chief boggle from the attic landing. "The gem must be through there."

Their footsteps squished and squelched up to

the door. Sophie and Sam huddled behind the shelves. Sophie mouthed: "One... two..."

The door swung open and the three Swamp Boggles came in.

"THREE!"

Sophie and Sam flicked the hairdryers on, and the loud whistling noise of the motors filled the attic. For a moment, the Swamp Boggles froze, almost comically surprised looks on their faces. Then they felt the warm air blowing on to their slimy skin.

"ARGH!" they shouted, jumping around.

They tried to turn about to get away from the blasts of air, but only succeeded in tripping over each other's feet and bumping heads. Sophie heard their skin cracking and saw her opportunity.

Leaving Sam to work the hairdryers, she jumped up and ran round towards the rapidly hardening boggles. "Take that! And that, you slimy slug brains!"

Her Guardian powers surged through her. Turning in mid-air, she kicked out with both feet. There was a loud *crunch* as the boggle she'd kicked staggered backwards. *Yes!* thought Sophie. If she could just knock them all over, then she could grab Sam and use her superspeed to whizz them downstairs!

Seeing the chief boggle lunging towards her, Sophie pivoted round and kicked his hands away. *Thud! Thwap!* Turning a back flip, she landed neatly on the floor. "Go on, make my day!" she declared, dusting her hands down as he came at her.

Then suddenly the hairdryers stopped.

Silence filled the room. Sophie swung round, her eyes wide with horror. The third boggle had reached the socket in the wall and pulled the hairdryers' plugs out!

The chief laughed. "Or maybe you can make *my* day!" He grabbed the cables of the hairdryers, pulling them hard so that the hairdryers jerked out of Sam's hands. The chief tossed them to Hissy Voice, who threw them outside the door. Already, Sophie could see the boggles's bodies getting squishier again as they refilled with slime and water.

"Uh-oh," said Sam as he scrambled to his

feet. With evil grins, the boggles formed a line and began approaching. *"Uh-oh" is right*, thought Sophie. *Now* what were they going to do?

As the boggles drew closer, Sam and Sophie backed off, Sophie almost tripping over her school bag. She grabbed it. Maybe there was something in it she could throw to keep them back? Not *The Shadow Files*, she couldn't risk losing that, but she had her school reading book and water bottle. Grabbing them she sent them flying through the air, but the boggles just ducked and kept on coming. Sophie flung her empty lunch box too, but that simply squished off the chief boggle's shoulder.

Sophie felt the wall behind her back. This was it – she and Sam couldn't go any further.

Beside her, Sam's face was pale. Then his foot

bumped into the painting of the girl and the kitten that he'd taken down off the shelf earlier. "Right, forget this!" he muttered, scooping it quickly up. "I'm not just going to stand here and be squelched by a Swamp Boggle! *Geronimo!*"

With a yell, he ran straight at the nearest one. Sophie watched in amazement as he slammed the painting down on the boggle's head. It popped out through the canvas and the boggle started to yell, then broke off as a sneeze ripped through it.

"*ATCHOO!*"

The boggle began to stagger about with the picture round his neck. "*ATCHOO! ATCHOO!*" Slimy green snot flew across the room.

Sophie's mouth was open as she gaped at the

scene. She had no idea why it was sneezing, but at least it was otherwise occupied now. "Way to go, Sam!" she cried, ducking to avoid the snot as it splatted into the wall behind her head.

The other two boggles started to sneeze too. They backed away from the painting.

"What are they doing?" cried Sophie.

"The question's not what are *they* doing, but what are *we* going to do, Soph?" Sam said wildly. "How are we going to get out of here?"

"I dunno! Where's Cutie-Pie when you need him?" Sophie reached into her bag and found her pencil case. She chucked that at the chief too, but it bounced harmlessly off his chest and that made him notice her again.

Snarling, the two boggles began to approach her and Sam once more, reaching out with their bony fingers. Sophie's heart pounded. How were they going to get out? She reached desperately into her bag, but the only thing left in there apart from *The Shadow Files* was the Fluffy. One of the boggles's mouths started opening. Maybe she could stuff the Fluffy into it! She pulled it out.

"ARGH!" shrieked the boggle immediately. He pointed at the Fluffy, his mouth opening and closing, strange, terrified gibbering noises coming from him.

"ARGH!" yelled the other two – even the one with the picture over its head!

The Fluffy blinked sweetly at them. "Me wanna cuddle!"

"No!" screeched the boggles. They started backing away, all suddenly sneezing violently.

"What's happening now?" Sam gasped to Sophie.

"I don't know!" Sophie said. "They don't seem to like the Fluffy, though." Her eyes widened as she spoke. The Fluffy... the picture of the girl and the kitten... Cutie-Pie... The Swamp Boggles didn't like anything cute! Why? She didn't know and right now, she didn't have time to think about it. She and Sam had to get out of the attic in whatever way they could.

She advanced, holding the Fluffy out in front of her like a sword. "Say hello to the Fluffy!" she sang at them.

"Mama! Me hungwy! Feed me!" Its mouth opened and closed, making hopeful sucking noises at the boggles.

"No! Please, no!" moaned the Swamp Boggles. Moving as one, they turned and raced for the doorway. Trying to get through all at once, they got stuck, kicking and pushing.

Sophie kept advancing.

"Wanna kiss-kiss!" The Fluffy made a kissing noise. The boggles's struggles grew

more intense. One managed to squeeze his way out and fled down the stairs, with the key in his hand. The other two were too busy fighting with each other to get away. Red spots started to pop out all over them, and between the shrieks they were still sneezing uncontrollably.

"They *really* don't like that Fluffy!" Sam said with a grin.

"They don't like anything cute!" gasped Sophie.

"In which case…" Sam grabbed a cricket bat and swiped at the mountain of Fluffy boxes. "Say hello to the Fluffy army!" he yelled.

The boxes exploded around the room, setting off the Fluffies' mechanisms. Suddenly the attic was full of the sound of Fluffy voices: "Feed me… Mama… kiss-kiss… cuddle…"

One landed right by the doorway. It waggled

its ears and looked up through its eyelashes at the two terrified boggles still stuck there. "Me wanna… wanna… WEE-WEE!" It squealed the last word.

Suddenly there were two muffled popping sounds, like two water bombs bursting one after the other.

Sophie and Sam yelled and jumped back as swampy green water swept over the floor. Sophie stared. The boggles were no longer trapped in the doorway – they'd gone!

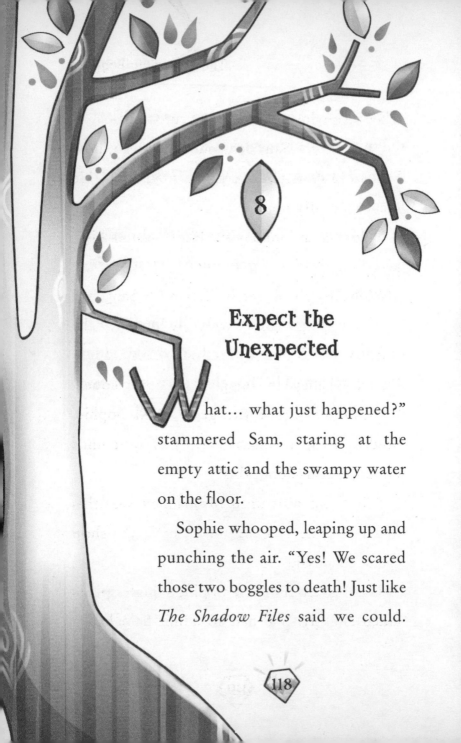

8

Expect the
Unexpected

"What... what just happened?" stammered Sam, staring at the empty attic and the swampy water on the floor.

Sophie whooped, leaping up and punching the air. "Yes! We scared those two boggles to death! Just like *The Shadow Files* said we could.

They're obviously terrified of cute things."

"But *why*?" Sam demanded. "I mean, how can a Fluffy frighten anyone to death?" He picked a Fluffy up.

It looked at him coyly. "Fluffy wanna kiss-kiss."

"OK, maybe I get it after all!" Sam said hastily putting it back down. He looked at the water on the floor again, and shook his head. "I just can't believe the boggles have really gone."

"*And* we've got the gem!" said Sophie, holding it up triumphantly. "Just wait until Grandpa hears about this!"

"And just wait until Mr Badgett sees this mess! He's never going to let us in the shop again," Sam said.

Gazing around her, Sophie's high spirits faded slightly. She had to admit Sam had a point. There were Fluffies and slimy water all over the floor, not to mention the broken picture and cricket bat. "You're right," she said. "We'd better get tidying."

"And fast!" agreed Sam.

Luckily, Grandpa and Mr Badgett took their time over their drink. By the time they got back, Sophie and Sam had just finished clearing away all the mess – including the slime trails the boggles had left downstairs.

"How's it going?" asked Mr Badgett as he and Grandpa came into the shop.

"Um... well, we haven't quite finished cleaning the attic yet," admitted Sophie, putting away the cloths and polish.

Sam nodded. "But we'll come back again another time and do the rest then, if that's OK."

"Oh, there is rather a lot of tidying to be done up there!" said Mr Badgett. "But any time you're passing and feel like earning a bit of extra money, just call in."

Sophie saw Grandpa looking around. She could tell his sharp eyes were taking in the damp patches on the floor where the slime had been. "We'd better be going," he said. "Don't want to be late for supper. Get your bags, you two."

Sophie fetched the carrier bag with the spray cans in it.

"See you soon, Jack," Grandpa said, ushering Sophie and Sam out of the door.

"Bye!" Sam and Sophie called over their shoulders.

"So?" Grandpa demanded in a low voice as they set off down the High Street. "What happened in there?"

They quickly told him everything, from spraying the boggles with the starch to finally defeating them. "But that's wonderful!" Grandpa exclaimed. "So you have the gem?"

"Yes! Got it right here!" Sophie patted her purse belt proudly.

"And the Swamp Boggles have really gone?"

"Vanished, turned into water," said Sam.

Grandpa looked stunned. "I can't believe it!"

Sophie grinned. "But, Grandpa, you know you must always expect the unexpected!" She heard Sam muffle a snort of laughter beside her.

Grandpa harrumphed, and didn't answer.

"We did OK, didn't we?" Sophie said, shooting him a look.

"Yes, you did very well." The grudging look left him and he smiled an unusually warm smile.

"Both of you. That was excellent work. Excellent work indeed."

Sophie couldn't hold back her grin as a rush of delight swept through her.

"So why *were* the Swamp Boggles so scared of the Fluffies?" Sam asked Grandpa.

"After what has just happened, I think that Swamp Boggles must be similar to Swamp Imps, who are all severely allergic to anything cute," said Grandpa. "I once saw a Swamp Imp sneeze itself into pieces when it caught sight of a little ginger kitten with a bow round its neck. Fluffies would no doubt cause a very severe reaction to a creature with such an allergy. The sight of one would be terrifying to a Swamp Boggle."

"And the sight of fifty would frighten them to death!" said Sophie.

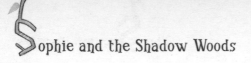

"Exactly."

"That must be why the Swamp Boggle ran off this morning!" realised Sam. "He was scared of Cutie-Pie, with his bow and sparkly collar!"

Sophie giggled. "Well, at least we'll know how to fight any swamp creatures from now on. We'll just set a cute little dog on them."

Grandpa didn't look amused. "One thing I'm sure about, the Ink Cap Goblins won't give up easily," he said. "The Swamp Boggles might have failed, but Ug will soon find some other shadow creatures to help him. We must find the other four gems as soon as we can."

"We will," Sophie promised. "We'll start looking through the files again tomorrow for more clues."

Sam met her eyes. "You know, that sounds like a job for…"

"*Book Boy!*" they whooped together. They both started laughing. Grandpa looked as if he thought they were completely mad, which made them laugh even more.

Still giggling, they went into the house. Mrs B and Anthony were in the kitchen. "These are for you," Sophie said, giving the carrier bag to Mrs B.

Mrs B looked inside. "*Three* cans of spray starch?"

"I didn't want us to run out," said Sophie innocently. "Starch can be *very* useful. I'm really sorry I used all yours up earlier." She gave Mrs B a hug.

Mrs B shook her head. "Oh, Sophie, sometimes I wonder what I'm going to do with you."

"Have her adopted?" Anthony said hopefully from the kitchen table.

Sophie pulled a face at him.

"Still got your Fluffy, sis?" he asked. "You wouldn't want to lose it now, would you?"

"No way!" said Sophie. She pulled the Fluffy out of her bag. Anthony gave a disgusted squawk as she swooped it at him, pretending to kiss his cheek. "It was the best present ever –

the absolute best! Thanks, Mrs B!"

Mrs B beamed, and Sophie grinned at the astonishment on her twin's face. "Come on, Sam." They ran upstairs to her room.

"What shadow creatures do you think Ug will send next time?" wondered Sam.

Sophie shuddered. "Nothing can be worse than Swamp Boggles!"

Sam looked at her. "Wolf Trolls?"

"No problem," she declared.

"Snake Sprites."

"Easy peasy."

"Bat Goblins?"

"We'd deal with them!"

Going over to the window, Sophie saw Grandpa practising Tai Chi in the garden. The Shadow Woods loomed up behind him. She smiled. Whatever creatures were waiting out there, she and Sam would be ready for them. "We'll get the key back and stop them finding the gems!" she vowed.

"Yeah," said Sam, joining her at the window. "We will. Book Boy and The Guardian – ready for anything!"

"Bring it on!" agreed Sophie with a grin.

In the Woods...

Deep in the woods, there was a loud yell that shook the branches of the trees. "Gah! Swamp Boggles! What do they think they're doing – dying on the job!" King Ug paced around his toadstool clearing, thwacking any goblin that came within reach. He had to get his

hands on one of the shadow gems! The key was useless otherwise – just a lump of old metal.

Suddenly an idea came into Ug's head. Slowly, he began to smile. Of course! He knew just what creature he was going to ask to help him next. He chortled in triumph, rubbing his pale hands together as the shadows in the woods darkened. Next time, that pesky girl Guardian wouldn't stand a chance!

THE
SHADOW
FILES

The King of the Ink Cap Goblins

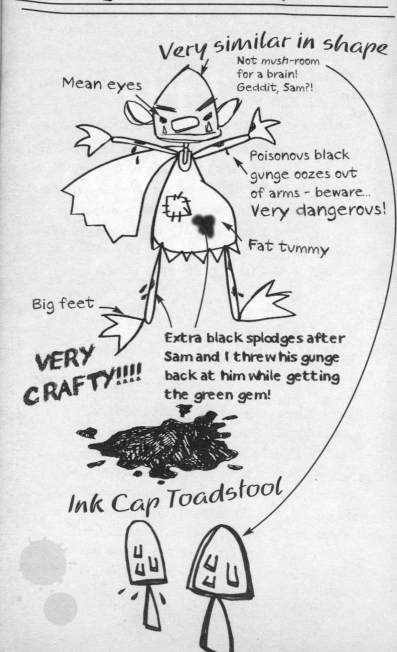

Very similar in shape

Not mush-room for a brain! Geddit, Sam?!

Mean eyes

Poisonous black gunge oozes out of arms - beware... Very dangerous!

Fat tummy

Big feet

VERY CRAFTY!!!!

Extra black splodges after Sam and I threw his gunge back at him while getting the green gem!

Ink Cap Toadstool

The Key to the Gateway

Hole for a gem from the Shadow Realm

Iron from the human world

The Key was forged by the first Guardian. It will only unlock and lock the gateway if a gem from the Shadow Realm is placed in the hole in the handle. BEWARE: The gateway must NEVER be opened!

THE GEMS

reen, yellow, red, blue, diamond, turquoise

Notes on the Gems: The first Guardian stole six gems from the Shadow Realm when he was making the key.

The gems are hidden separately from the key to make sure that even if the key is stolen, the shadow creatures will not be able to open the gateway. The shadow creatures must not get their hands on the gems for it is believed that if all six gems are ever taken into the Shadow Woods, dangerous Shadow Magic will ignite.

When the key comes near to a gem it glows so it can be used to find the gems.

Thunder Trolls

Beware the sharp spiny teeth! Used for attacking and defending

Beware the feet for when stamped they may cause peals of thunder to crash from the heavens and the ground to shake violently

probably very smelly!

The Thunder Troll is a very rare shadow creature; the last known specimen was sighted in 1842. The Thunder Troll shares the characteristics of the rest of the troll family, being fearless and savage.

CLUE ALERT!

High in an old place

The yellow gem can be found

Hidden on a dusty shelf

Strange wares all around.

SLIME TROLLS

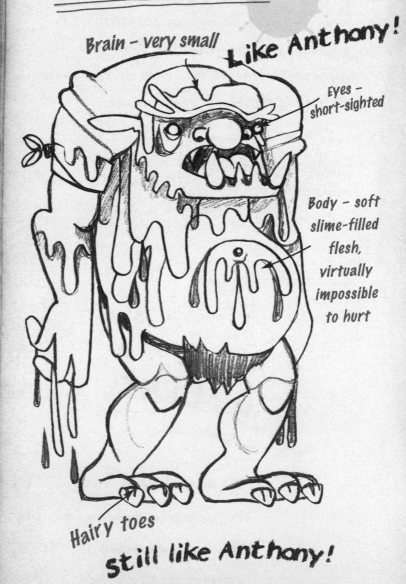

Brain – very small

Like Anthony!

Eyes – short-sighted

Body – soft slime-filled flesh, virtually impossible to hurt

Hairy toes

Still like Anthony!

Slime Troll Habitat and Habits

Slime Trolls like to live alone in caves or swamps. They amuse themselves by picking at their toes and seeing how much slime they can squeeze out of their belly button. They are generally vegetarian, eating toadstools and rotten tree bark.

That is so GROSS!

Defeating a Slime Troll

To fight a Slime Troll, one must first dry out their skin through use of wind or heat for then they will become vulnerable to blows and kicks.

Drain Danger!

BEWARE OF DRAINS! Some shadow creatures can use them to skulk around town in. They can possibly even come up through the toilets - **eurgh!**

Solutions??

1. Jump on drains to slam lids back down on their heads.
2. Keep toilet lids shut AT ALL TIMES.
3. Go into the drains ourselves, to keep an eye on them?

NO WAY!!

SHADOW CREATURES - O US - 2!

Skin dried out and flaky from our attacks

Black spots from having goo flung back at him

Miserable looks because they STILL don't have a shadow gem!

Expect the unexpected!

BRING IT ON!

What's next in store for Sophie?

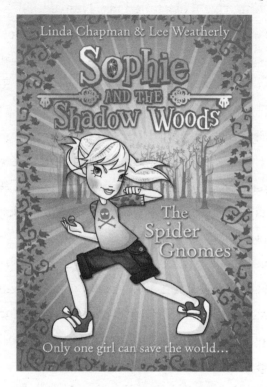

Linda Chapman & Lee Weatherly

Sophie
AND THE
Shadow Woods

The Spider Gnomes

Only one girl can save the world…

Deep in the Shadow Woods stood King Ug, the leader of the Ink Cap Goblins. His ivy crown rested wonkily on his dome-shaped head and his white flaky skin was covered with black blotches. He was talking to two squat figures in the shadows.

"Well? Do you think you can get one?" he demanded.

"Yessss," one of the figures hissed, waving four of its eight legs. "We shall find a shadow gem, no matter what."

"Those idiot Swamp Boggles said the same thing," snorted King Ug. "They failed me. Numskulls!"

There was the sound of snapping jaws. "Ah, but *we* shall not fail you. We know how important it is that we shadow creatures all serve you, King Ug – you are the Keeper of the Key!"

King Ug smiled proudly. The key to the gate hung round his chest, and he reached up and touched it, feeling the empty space where a shadow gem needed to go. "How will you manage to get into the town unseen?" he demanded.

There was the sound of leg joints cracking. "We have many spiessss with many eyessss," said one of the figures. A line of tiny spiders marched past on the ground. "They will search the humans' town and find a gem for us, and when they do we shall fetch it and bring it here. Nothing shall stop usss!"

"Excellent!" chortled King Ug. He adjusted his crown. "I can see it was extremely clever of me to call on the Spider Gnomes for help. When you succeed, the gem will be mine and I shall finally open the gate." His small black eyes gleamed as he imagined the fun that millions of shadow creatures would have, wreaking havoc in the human world.

All he needed was one small gem...

"Do you have what it takes to be the NEXT GUARDIAN?"

Prove your worth for a chance to win AWESOME prizes!
It's simple and fun!

Read the *Sophie and the Shadow Woods* series
Answer three questions about each book
Pass a stage, collect a gem, enter for great prizes/freebies
Pass SIX stages and get entered into the grand prize draw!

Stage Two

Answer these simple questions about *The Swamp Boggles*:

1. Where was the yellow gem hidden?
2. What did Sophie and Sam use to dry out the Swamp Boggles?
3. Who is Book Boy?

Got the answers? Go to:
www.sophieandtheshadowwoods.com
and start your journey!

You can find Stage One in *The Goblin King* and look out for Stage Three in *The Spider Gnomes*, out in July.

Good Luck!